With love for Crash Bang Mark Barrett.
J. N.

First published in Great Britain in 2010 by
Gullane Children's Books
185 Fleet Street, London, EC4A 2HS
www.gullanebooks.com

1   3   5   7   9   10   8   6   4   2

Text and illustrations © Jill Newton 2010

ISBN: 978-1-86233-720-6

Printed and bound in China

Crash Bang Donkey!

Jill Newton

GULLANE
CHILDREN'S BOOKS

Farmer Gruff was a very happy man. There was just one
thing wrong . . . Day and night, the crows munched and
crunched on the corn in the cornfield, and day and
night, Farmer Gruff had to chase them away.

Now he needed sleep, and he needed it badly! And while he slept,
the animals made not a peep. The lambs skipped silently in the meadow,
the pigs rolled silently in the mud and the chickens laid eggs silently
in the henhouse. There was not a sound to be heard, until . . .

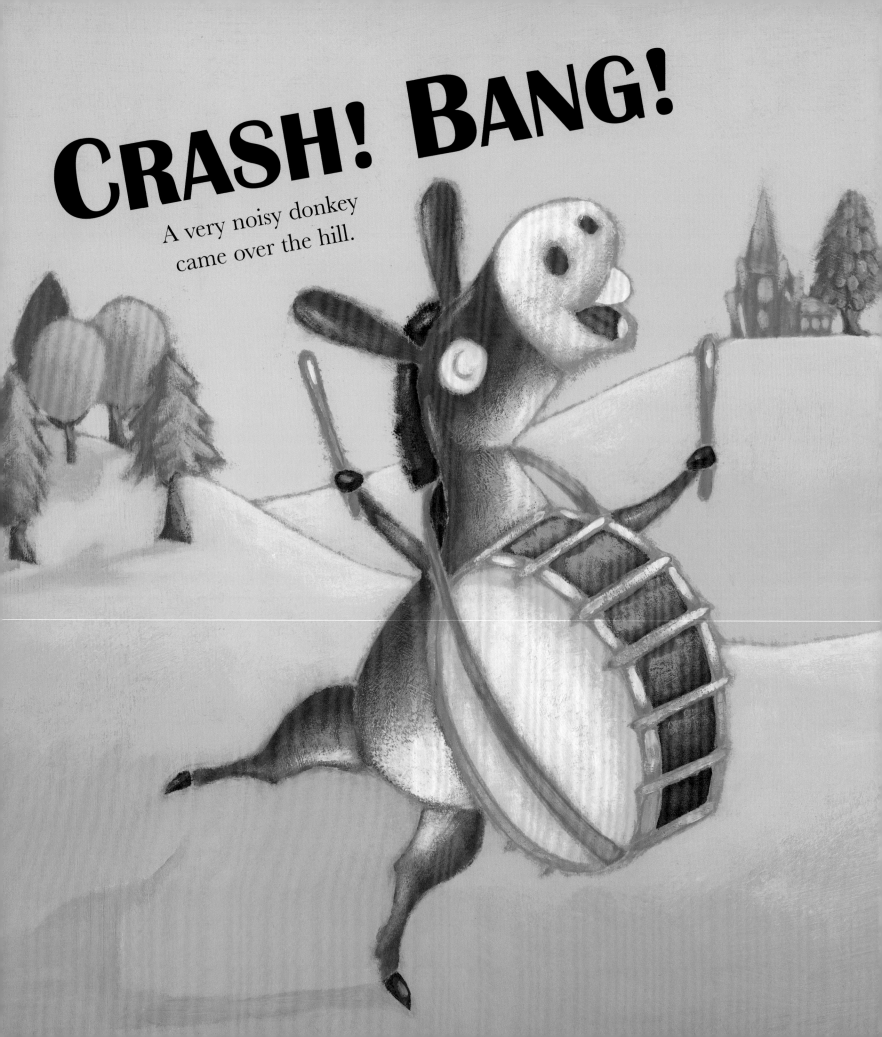

CRASH! BANG!

A very noisy donkey
came over the hill.

"shush!"

whispered Pig
and Lamb and Chicken.
"Farmer Gruff is trying to sleep.
Your crashing and banging
will wake him up!"

But Donkey was making so
much noise he couldn't
hear them. He took out
his trumpet, and . . .

PARP!

he went.
"Please stop!"
clucked Chicken.
But Donkey *still*
couldn't hear.

PLINK PLONK PLONK PLINK!

"Come on, Pigster, feel the groove!

"Ride the rhythm, baby!"

Then **POP!** Lamb pulled the plug out.
"Hey dude, what's occurring?" cried Donkey.
"Aren't you digging my sounds?"
"You're making too much noise!" said Lamb.
"Farmer Gruff is asleep!"

"OK, guys, I hear you," smiled
Donkey, and with a
Tra la la
he played a lullaby on his flute.
It didn't bang and it didn't crash . . .

But it was too late – Farmer
Gruff wasn't asleep any more.
"Who's making all that
NOISE?" he yelled.
"Hey, Farmer G," said Donkey.
"That would be me. I'm
Crash Bang Donkey and I'm
here to play my music . . .

". . . to blow
on the saxophone,
shake the maracas,
clash those castanets, and
bash those tom-toms . . .

"Get in the groove, Gruffy!
It'll do you good!"

"I haven't got time
for music, Donkey,"
shouted Farmer Gruff.
"The crows are making a meal
of my corn and YOU are making
me mad. Put that noise back in
your bag – and LEAVE!"

So Donkey left.

The animals went back to their quiet day, and Farmer Gruff
went back to sleep. But it wasn't long before there was a
CRASH BANG! CRASH BANG! coming from the barn.
"Oh no!" gasped Chicken and Pig and Lamb.
"Donkey's at it again!"

And then they noticed the crows. They were
flapping and squawking. Crash Bang Donkey
was scaring them off the corn!

CRASH!
BANG!

Chicken, Pig and Lamb peered round the barn door.
"What's up?" exclaimed Donkey. "Was I too loud?
Did I make too much noise?"
"Oh no!" grinned Pig.
"You made just the right amount
of noise," chuckled Chicken.
"I'm going to fetch Farmer Gruff!"
said Lamb excitedly.

Donkey looked worried.

But when Farmer Gruff saw the crows flapping and squawking, a large smile spread across his face. "You can stay here after all, Donkey," he said. "But you don't like my music!" said Donkey. "Neither do the crows," said Farmer Gruff, "and what they don't like makes me VERY happy indeed. Please play your music as loudly as you can, from sunrise to sunset."

And from that day forward, the crows didn't go anywhere near the corn, and Farmer Gruff got lots of sleep – especially when Donkey played him the occasional lullaby!